MW01077102

TUMFORD'S RUDE NOISES

Nancy Tillman

FEIWEL AND FRIENDS

NEW YORK

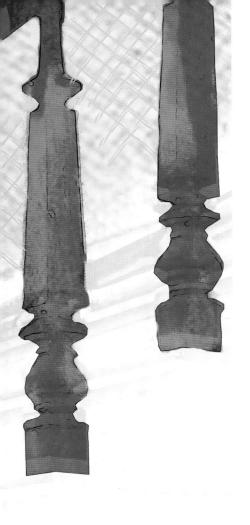

Tumford Stoutt, like most little boys,
liked to be silly and liked to make noise.
It didn't matter that he was a cat.
(Tum never bothered with details like that.)

But today, Tum's parents
were not in the mood.
He wasn't just loud.
Tumford was rude!

As everyone knows,
(if not, here's fair warning)
loud noise is not pleasant
first thing in the morning.

Yet early this Tuesday
in Sweet Apple Green,
Tum was an utter noise-making machine!

Face in his bowl, he blew bubbles and slurped.

Eating his sweet roll, he giggled and burped.

His parents not pleased,
were, in fact, quite put out
with the sum of rude noises
that came from Tum Stoutt.

You'd think that would stop him.
But, no! Not a bit.
In fact, Tumford got
quite a thrill out of it!

There's one tiny thing
that perhaps I should mention. . . .

Sometimes, he did these
things just for attention.

Dear! That meant trouble
indeed for Tum Stoutt.
And he was certainly
soon to find out!

The Sweet Apple Guild,
expected at eight,
had just at this twinkling
marched in through the gate.

Can you imagine what Tumford Stoutt did?

That's right, you guessed it!
Heaven forbid!

Time seemed to stop,
at least for a minute.

But Tum didn't find much
to laugh about in it.

No, all he heard was the
loud voice of doom.

!! @ #%

"Take that ill-mannered cat out of the room!"

Bother and misery!
Poor Tumford Stoutt
had managed to land himself square in

TIME-OUT!

As everyone knows, loud sounds and rude noise
are not always welcome from small girls and boys.

They may get attention. It's true, yes they may.
But it won't be felt in a very nice way.

I'm sure that YOU could have told Tumford that.
Maybe you'd still like to help the poor cat.

Whisper these words in Tum's ear if you would. . . .
"Tumford . . . not all attention is good."

Look! Tummy heard you,
he heard loud and clear!
What a relief! Well done, my dear!

In Sweet Apple Green, the joy was so big
that everyone danced a quick Tumford Stoutt jig.

Now, there was no need for Tum's folks to scold him.
He'd learned his lesson . . . you'd already told him!

But, just to show that they both understood
that no one can ever be perfectly good,
the Stoutts promised Tum he could sometimes be silly,
as long as in private, and not willy-nilly.

So Tum with a grin mostly sweet and sincere,
made a rude little noise into Georgy's left ear.

And the Stoutts loved him madly from whiskers to toes,
just like I love you . . .

as everyone knows.

To my faithful friend and agent, Cathy (CathyPants) Hemming.—N.T.

A FEIWEL AND FRIENDS BOOK
An Imprint of Macmillan

TUMFORD'S RUDE NOISES. Copyright © 2012 by Nancy Tillman. All rights reserved. Printed in China by South China Printing Co. Ltd., Dongguan City, Guangdong Province. For information, address Feiwel and Friends, 175 Fifth Avenue, New York, N.Y. 10010.

Library of Congress Cataloging-in-Publication Data Available

ISBN: 978-0-312-36841-8

Book design by Nancy Tillman and Kathleen Breitenfeld

Feiwel and Friends logo designed by Filomena Tuosto

First Edition: 2012

10 9 8 7 6 5 4 3 2 1

mackids.com

You are loved.